LEGAL EAGLES

Newly qualified solicitor Helen Martin has just moved to a new area to start a job in an old-fashioned family firm, hoping to escape the problems of her past. Here she meets Peter, who has a story of his own; but they soon discover that the past has a habit of throwing obstacles in the way. And while the senior partner of Helen's firm struggles when his estranged son reappears, it seems that the lovebirds' paths might already be more intertwined than they could have imagined . . .

REBECCA HOLMES

LEGAL EAGLES

Complete and Unabridged

LINFORD
Leicester

First published in Great Britain in 2017

First Linford Edition
published 2020

A catalogue record for this book is available
from the British Library.

ISBN 978–1–4448–4485–6

Published by
Ulverscroft Limited
Anstey, Leicestershire

Set by Words & Graphics Ltd.
Anstey, Leicestershire
Printed and bound in Great Britain by
T. J. International Ltd., Padstow, Cornwall

This book is printed on acid-free paper

1

Helen Martin could have sworn she'd slept only a matter of minutes before her alarm clock jolted her out of a sequence of uneasy dreams.

She had spent most of the night tossing and turning, apprehension battling with excitement about the day ahead, practically giving up on the idea of getting any sleep before she'd finally nodded off.

It took all her willpower not to burrow further under the bedclothes, but instead step out into her bedroom, cold without the gas fire lit, and head for the bathroom, crossing her fingers that a shower would help her wake up properly.

Twenty minutes later, dressed, hair combed and with a dab of make-up applied in record time, Helen was in the kitchen, drinking coffee as hot as she could stand it and thinking that, like its cousin the pot, a watched toaster never toasted.

The sound of another bedroom door opening in the draughty old house was followed by the pad of slippered feet coming down the stairs before Jackie, her housemate, appeared.

She barely seemed to have her eyes open as she pulled her dressing-gown more tightly round herself and knotted the cord.

'Morning.' A yawn all but drowned out her greeting. 'I was on a late shift.'

Since moving into the house a couple of days before, Helen had met Jackie twice. On both occasions, there had only been time for the briefest of chats, with Jackie either being on her way out to work or just in from a long shift and ready to collapse into bed.

They'd managed to exchange basic details about jobs and where they were from, and agree how cold it was.

As a result Helen knew Jackie was a nurse at the local infirmary, but little else apart from the fact that she supported the local football team.

That had been enough to create a mutual sense that they would get along as housemates. Only time would tell whether a deeper friendship grew from there.

Overall, Helen was aware she had a lot to be grateful for. The house might not be luxurious, but compared to some of the places she had stayed in as a student it was a palace, situated in a leafy suburb with a little garden at the front and back.

The swirly carpets and orange curtains, throwbacks to the 1970s, were not to everyone's taste, but the woodchip wallpaper looked as if it had been painted recently and the new electric kettle meant they didn't have to wait ages for the old tin one on the gas cooker to come to the boil.

If only the same could be said for the toaster. It was tempting not to bother, but Helen's mother had always impressed upon her the importance of having some form of breakfast.

'You off?' Jackie, more awake now, brought her back to the moment.

Helen nodded and took a last gulp of the coffee, gasping as the heat of the liquid caught her unaware.

'Nervous?' Jackie asked.

'Just a bit.'

'You'll be fine. I wanted to be up in time to wish you luck. There was something else, as well.' Jackie put one hand to her forehead, remembering. 'You know that empty bedroom? Apparently it won't be empty for much longer.

'I was going to tell you when I got in last night, but wasn't sure whether your light was still on.'

'It probably wasn't,' Helen called as she rushed into the hall and shrugged on her coat. 'I was getting an early night. Not that that was much use.'

Coming back into the kitchen, she retrieved the toast and spread some margarine on it before glancing at her watch.

'I'd love to hear more but I have four minutes to get to the bus stop. See you later.'

She grabbed her bag, keys and toast and ran into the cold morning.

Despite being hampered by her office clothes and smart shoes, she made it to the bus stop with half a minute to spare, and just finished eating her toast as the bus lumbered into view.

The three other people at the stop stepped towards the kerb. Helen followed while trying to organise her bag, fumbling with the zip-up compartment at the back for her keys.

At the same time, she got out her purse ready to count out change, not sure how much the fare was and not wanting to annoy an impatient driver with a note.

The zip was stuck. Trying to hook the keyring over her finger while not letting money tip out of her purse, she felt it slide before she could do anything about it, followed by the clink of metal hitting tarmac.

The first two passengers had already stepped on to the bus, but the third, a middle-aged lady, was still at ground level.

She and Helen narrowly avoided bumping heads as they bent down at the same time. The lady handed the keys over with a smile.

'Thank you. I'm such a butterfingers this morning. It's my first day in a new job,' Helen explained.

'Judging by your clothes, I take it you're going to be working in an office?'

'That's right.' They both stepped on to the bus as the passenger in front handed over his fare and moved on. 'At Barnes and Son, near the town centre.'

'The solicitors? They're an old firm. Well respected, too. You'll polish up your typing skills there, all right. Forty-two, please,' the lady told the driver.

'Good luck,' she added to Helen. 'You'll be fine once you've got your first day out of the way.'

'Thank you.' Helen concentrated on checking the fare with the driver and finding a seat, only just keeping her balance as the bus lurched as she made her way down the aisle.

As she sat down, she wondered

whether she should have corrected the lady's assumption that she was going to work as a secretary, but decided against it.

It was a common enough mistake to make. Besides, dropping one's keys at a bus stop could hardly be regarded as promising behaviour for a solicitor.

⋆ ⋆ ⋆

Margaret Hall lifted the cover from her typewriter. This part of the morning was her favourite time. Even with the extra organisation involved, it was worth making the effort to get to work early.

Mind you, she thought, 'extra organisation' was probably a bit of an understatement.

Although she just had one teenager left at home to deal with nowadays, and a slightly bumbling but well-meaning husband, breakfast times still had plenty of potential for chaos.

It helped that, as long-standing secretary to the senior partner, she had her own office, complete with filing cabinets and a large desk with drawers to keep everything in order.

The room was spacious, yet not too big. The window looked out on to a quiet street of Edwardian brick buildings occupied by similar businesses. All in all, it was perfect for a few minutes' calm to gain focus before the switchboard at reception opened and the day began in earnest.

The shrill ring of the internal phone, followed by the authoritative tone of Clarence Barnes, brought her to attention.

'Margaret. Would you pop down to my office?'

'I'll be right there, Mr Clarence.'

She picked up a notepad and sharpened pencil, in case he should decide to kill two birds with one stone and dictate a few letters while she was there.

He often joked that he was the one who struggled to keep up with her shorthand, rather than the other way round.

After knocking and entering the ground floor office, tucked away behind reception so that Mr Clarence could be aware of all the goings-on, she saw a young girl with light brown hair and a pale complexion perched on a chair in front of the huge mahogany desk.

The senior partner leaned back in a leather swivel chair on the other side.

'Good morning, Margaret. I'd like you to meet Miss Helen Martin, our new solicitor. She's been qualified for about six months and gained invaluable experience at her previous firm, where she served her two years as an articled clerk before qualifying, so I'm sure she will be a very useful member of the team.'

'Hello.' The newcomer gave a small smile in her direction.

Maybe her complexion wasn't usually so pale, Margaret surmised.

Anyone would think she and Mr Clarence were ogres, the way some people reacted when they first came here.

Young Karen, for instance, had been

timid as a mouse for her first few weeks. Heaven only knew how they'd have reacted to old Mr Barnes. Even Margaret had been scared of him.

It was difficult to believe that a slip of a girl like this could be up to coping in a male-dominated profession.

Margaret smiled politely and nodded her acknowledgement.

'I've been telling Helen that you're worth your weight in gold, and that if she has any questions regarding how this office is run, you're the one with all the answers.' Mr Clarence paused as there was a knock at the door. 'That will be Karen, our junior secretary. I've asked her to show you around.'

Once Clarence and Margaret had the room to themselves, her boss slumped back in his chair.

'More changes, though I suppose it's for the best. I can't help wondering what my father would have made of it.

'I like to imagine he'd have been forward-thinking enough to have agreed. I'd almost forgotten that Miss Martin was starting today. These past two weeks have been a blur.'

Margaret cleared her throat.

'How was your mother's funeral? Several clients phoned on Friday to pass on their respects.'

They had debated whether to close the office for the day of the funeral, but concluded that business should continue as normally as possible. Margaret, though invited, had sensed she was needed to hold the fort.

Mr Clarence smiled sadly.

'It was a good service, if that's the right description. I read out her favourite Robert Frost poem and the minister gave a worthy eulogy. The chapel was full.

'Friends and relatives came from all over the world — including James, who travelled from Australia. Well, he could hardly not for his own mother's funeral.' He hesitated. 'My son was there, too.'

Margaret placed her notebook and pencil on the desk and leaned forward slightly.

'How is he? Is he coming home?'

Clarence put the ends of his fingers together to form a steeple.

'I only saw him across the room at the wake afterwards. Eleanor and Samantha went to talk to him. They seemed pleased to see each other.

'He can never do anything wrong in Eleanor's eyes, and Samantha's always adored her big brother.'

He sat up straight and opened a file.

'He's not coming home, or at least not to my knowledge, and certainly not until he sees sense. If things had gone to plan, he would be here in this office, following in mine and my father's footsteps, instead of dropping out of his law degree then going off the way he did.

'It's all very well saying it wasn't for him, but he let the family down,' he continued. 'We can't all afford that sort of luxury. At some stage he's going to need to earn a decent living.'

He sighed impatiently.

'He's turning out to be just like his

uncle James. Remember how much upset that caused?'

Margaret did, and she'd heard the story many times. Every family had its problems. Every action had its ramifications.

'He'll find his own path in life,' she said. 'It takes some people a little longer, that's all. Do you remember how Arthur and I were worried about Adam?

'He was always falling out with his dad, too. Then he joined the Army and that seemed to straighten him out. Thankfully, Alison seems to be easier to cope with.'

Family matters over with, they both seemed equally glad to get on to the safer topic of work.

Margaret took some dictation before carrying an armful of files to her office to deal with.

As she slotted carbon paper between two sheets and fed them into her typewriter, she wondered what it was about men that made it so difficult for some of them to get along. Pride? Some primaeval need to show who was in charge?

It reminded her of those Argentinian scrap metal merchants who had been on the news the other day, planting a flag on an island in the middle of the ocean. What was the point of that, other than idle posturing?

Mind, Mr Clarence had seemed to think there was more to it than met the eye when they discussed it during their usual few minutes' morning chat.

His instinct was often right, certainly when it came to his clients, but in Margaret's view they might as well be peacocks, strutting around showing off their feathers.

* * *

'Don't be put off by Mrs Hall,' Karen told Helen once the door to the senior partner's office was closed and they were in reception. 'She's not bad once you get used to her.'

Pam, the receptionist, nodded in agreement.

'She likes things done her way and

expects the place to run like clockwork. She worships Mr Clarence. They've been working together for over twenty-five years.'

Pam turned back to the switchboard as a call came in.

'Why do people call him Mr Clarence?' Helen asked Karen.

Karen giggled.

'It's a habit from the past, so people didn't get him mixed up with his father and brother, Mr Barnes and Mr James.

'Mr James didn't stay very long. It was before my time, but apparently he was a bit of a black sheep and emigrated to Australia.

'Mrs Hall remembers him but doesn't say much, though she did let it slip once that he used to make everyone laugh. It's hard to imagine Mr Clarence doing that.

'Mr Barnes senior retired a few years ago and died of a heart attack shortly afterwards. Apparently he ruled with an iron rod and everyone was terrified of him.'

By now they were in Karen's office,

which doubled as a store room, judging by the cardboard boxes of stationery stacked up against one wall.

A manual typewriter took pride of place on a wooden table, with a more modest swivel chair than the one in Mr Clarence's room. Two wire baskets of files with small dictation tapes on top stood to one side.

Karen nodded towards them.

'I mainly work for one of the other solicitors, Paul, but I'll also be doing your typing until your workload builds up. At that stage Mrs Hall will decide what to do for you, secretary-wise.'

They walked back through reception and along a short corridor into the largest room yet, with a musty yet comforting odour of old books on floor to ceiling shelves.

'This is the library, where the various law journals and reference books are kept if you need to look something up. Old files are kept in the cellar. You use the door under the stairs to get there.' Karen looked thoughtful.

'I suppose this must seem very different for you compared to the last place you worked. Weren't you in a big city centre firm?'

'That's right,' Helen replied, finally able to get a word in edgeways. Apart from Mrs Hall, people around here seemed very chatty.

'It was slap bang in the centre and had twelve partners, all leading their own specialist departments. The phones never stopped ringing, and all the partners were known by their first name.'

She didn't add that clients were dealt with quickly and at arm's length, nor that there was a high staff turnover as individuals moved on to their next goal.

They would probably regard somewhere like this with horror, seeing it as a backwater where everyone seemed happy to stagnate in one place.

'That sounds exciting, not to mention handy for the shops, but I'm not sure I'd like it. You've moved a long way, as well, haven't you? I'd hate to move so far. My boyfriend wouldn't be keen. Are you seeing anyone?' Karen asked.

'No,' Helen replied shortly.

She looked intently at a shelf containing bound volumes of 'The All England Law Reports'. The last thing she wanted to do was talk about her private life.

'Well, maybe that's for the best. Long-distance relationships can be a pain, and Mr Clarence wouldn't appreciate you being distracted from your job by problems like that.

'I'm sure you'll find someone soon. There are plenty of nice men around.'

'Are you talking about me again?'

They both looked round as a tall man of about thirty, with sandy hair and a friendly grin, strode into the room. He held his hand out to her.

'You must be Helen. I'm Paul, one of the other solicitors here, mainly specialising in wills. There are four of us in all, now that you've joined. Welcome to the firm.

'You'll find we're a friendly bunch, if a bit odd at times,' he teased. 'And don't worry — I'm taken. As for you . . .'

18

he turned to Karen and adopted a mock stern expression '. . . you can stop your matchmaking and get those fingers flying. I've left another tape for you.'

He grinned again.

'I'll catch up with you later. I've got a client coming in who wants to change their will. Again. I wonder who he's fallen out with this time?' He chuckled.

'He seems like a nice bloke,' Helen commented once he was gone.

'He is,' Karen agreed. 'He even teases Mrs Hall and makes her smile.' She sighed. 'I'd better get on. Will you be OK?'

'I'll be fine. I've got some files I need to start reading in my office upstairs, so that should keep me occupied for the rest of the morning.'

'Do you think you'll like it here?' Karen asked.

'It looks promising.'

And it did, Helen reflected as she settled at her desk. She felt less apprehensive than she had earlier. So long as people didn't ask too many questions, it looked as if making a fresh start had been a good plan.

★ ★ ★

At half past six, Clarence Barnes decided to call it a day. Although that was early for him, he was still the last person in the office.

Paul had left half an hour before, most of the other staff at five fifteen, and he'd heard the new girl let herself out just after five thirty.

It made a welcome change to be able to travel home in daylight, heading through the outskirts of the town he'd known all his life, and on towards the moors.

This was the country he loved, satisfyingly bleak and beautiful in its own way.

Of course, he knew that not everyone saw it like that, including his wife, Eleanor, hailing originally as she did from a gentler landscape further south.

But even Eleanor adored their old farmhouse. The views from its windows were a heart-lifting sight, even in the wildest weather, and the sense of space always helped him think.

Dusk was falling as he drove up the track. The house looked solid and reassuring, with lights glowing from the windows, like the final beacons before the darkening hills beyond.

No sooner had he opened the front door than he was greeted by his daughter, Samantha, and Pip, the family's black Labrador.

'Dad! You're early.'

Clarence was almost thrown off balance as Sam threw her arms around him.

She'd taken her grandmother's death particularly hard and over the last few days that had translated into shows of physical affection.

He himself had never been demonstrative, but if this helped his daughter to cope, then he was happy to go along with it.

'How was school?' he asked once she'd released him.

She grimaced.

'OK. I've got tons of French homework.'

It was no secret that the select girls' school Samantha attended in the next town put great store in intensive study, but that was the price one paid for a top-level education. Clarence had had to go through the same at that age.

'Vanessa phoned,' Sam added. 'She says there's a spare horse for the show-jumping class on Saturday, and it's mine if I want it. Mum said I should check with you. Can I go?'

Vanessa, the owner of the local riding stables, had had a lot of success in various equestrian competitions and was worshipped by his horse-mad daughter.

As the stables had such a high reputation, the lessons cost an arm and a leg, but Sam enjoyed them.

'Go on, then. Your mum will have to give you a lift, though. I've got a lot of work to catch up on.'

'Thanks, Dad. You're the best.'

As she skipped back into the

living-room, Clarence glanced after her. A row of sympathy cards lined the mantelpiece.

There were more on top of the piano, too, as if to remind him that he hadn't imagined recent events.

The sound of footsteps on the hall's oak flooring announced Eleanor emerging from the kitchen.

'Two more cards arrived today,' she told him after they kissed briefly in greeting. 'One from a cousin of your mother's in Canada. And one from Peter.'

'Nice of him,' Clarence said tightly. 'If late.'

'He had a lot to do in the week before the funeral. He was on the move, remember. At least he came. That can't have been easy for him.'

'He still kept his distance from me.'

'Can you blame him after the last conversation you two had? And then nothing for the five years since? It's like your father and brother all over again.

'They never made up, even to your father's dying day. Is that what you want with your own son?'

Clarence struggled to keep his voice low.

'As I've said before, you weren't there at the time. James threw everything away and left us in the lurch. He left me carrying the can.'

'Maybe, but your mother told me how it almost tore her in two.' Eleanor put her hand on his arm. 'Why are you doing this to yourself, Clarence? It's all very well having a sense of duty, but you can take it too far.'

'Because these things are important. If Peter had an ounce of — '

He stopped as he noticed Eleanor glance behind him.

'There's a delicious smell coming from the kitchen,' Samantha said brightly.

'That'll be the casserole,' her mother replied.

Clarence frowned.

'It's quarter past seven. Haven't you normally eaten by now?'

'We're running late. We went to the new out-of-town supermarket. You wouldn't believe the range they've got there. We'll need a bigger freezer.'

'I'll take your word for it. By the way,' he added to Sam with a wink, 'we had a young lady solicitor starting today. You'll probably meet her at the summer barbecue. She might be able to give you a few tips for when it's your turn.'

'Oh. OK.'

'Dinner's nearly ready.' Eleanor interrupted.

Clarence grunted as he lifted up his bulging briefcase.

'I'll take mine to the study.'

Samantha's face fell.

'Why don't you eat with us?'

'Because I've got a lot to do, including sorting out your gran's estate.'

To his surprise, both his wife and daughter blocked his path. Pip, sensing the prospect of a game, danced round his feet.

'It can wait for another evening,' Eleanor said. 'You're eating with us, and that's final.'

The meal turned out to be thoroughly

enjoyable. Eleanor opened a bottle of wine which the two of them finished afterwards as they all watched a film rented from the video library in the town centre.

When Clarence mentioned a documentary he wanted to record, it was Sam who set the timer.

'We should do this more often,' Eleanor told him. 'Your life's in danger of being all work and no play.'

But Clarence had dozed off, so wasn't able to reply.

★   ★   ★

On Friday morning, reluctant to wake to her alarm after a long week, Helen clicked it over to the radio setting in the hope of some cheerful music to help her get moving.

When she heard an announcement that it was seven o'clock and here were the news headlines, her drowsy consciousness picked up that the reporter's voice sounded grave. Why did they always concentrate on bad news?

She forced her eyes open and switched off the radio.

In the kitchen, the aroma of Jackie's toast made the room feel warmer and welcoming by association, along with the background music of the radio on the small, melamine-topped table.

It was the first time Helen had seen her since Monday, due to a combination of her housemate's work shifts and the fact that she seemed to go out quite a lot with friends.

She wondered how long it would be before she knew enough people to have a social life again.

Arguably, she only had herself to blame for that, but evenings were lonely at the moment and no-one at work seemed a likely candidate.

'How's the new job?' Jackie asked.

'Tiring, but it's getting there,' Helen replied. 'It's different from my last place. I think I'll like it once I've settled in.'

Helen retrieved her toast from the

toaster and spread jam on it. Having got her morning routine more organised, she now had time for a quick breakfast in the house rather than on the way to the bus stop.

Over the weekend she would sort out a food shopping trip and find her feet in the area generally.

'I'm sorry I had to rush out on Monday. Any more on the new housemate?' she asked.

'No. I only know what the landlord told me when he called round to collect the rent. Hopefully they'll be nice. Oh, is it seven-thirty already?'

Jackie stopped talking as more news headlines came on the radio, making Helen wonder if there was any escape from them.

As they listened, Helen could hardly believe her ears. Argentinian ships were approaching somewhere called the Falkland Islands, which apparently were British, and an invasion was expected within hours.

It seemed some kind of defence force

was being mustered and islanders had been urged to stay indoors.

Jackie breathed in sharply.

'I don't like the sound of that.'

'Neither do I. I'm ashamed to have to ask this, but where are the Falkland Islands?'

'I'm not sure.'

It was a relief when a Duran Duran record came on. They both hummed along with no idea of the reaction to the news in a house on the other side of town.

★   ★   ★

In that house, a couple of miles away, Margaret was struggling to start her day.

For reasons she couldn't explain, she'd slept badly. Her grandmother used to say that she always had a feeling when something wrong was in the air, and that stopped her sleeping.

No sooner had the memory come to her than Margaret gave herself a shake

29

and dismissed it. She was a firm believer in good old common sense.

Besides, what women with family and work responsibilities didn't have a bad night's sleep every now and then?

The radio presenter's good-natured chatter in between the music provided a comforting background to the clatter of spoons against cereal bowls and the spreading of marmalade.

She was hoping they didn't play anything too noisy this morning when Alison came into the kitchen, looking flustered.

'Mum, I need some socks for my PE kit. The others got wet at cross-country on Tuesday and there aren't clean ones in my drawer.'

Margaret rolled her eyes.

'You'll find some in the airing cupboard. Put the dirty ones in the laundry basket.'

'Thanks, Mum. I'll — '

'Shush!' The conversation was cut off by Arthur.

Margaret hadn't realised it was time for the news headlines. She froze as a serious-sounding voice cut across the stillness of the room.

It was saying something about Royal Marines and local volunteers, and that an invasion was expected within hours.

'Where's that?' Alison asked.

'The Falkland Islands.' Arthur replied.

'Are they near Britain?'

'No, but they're British territory, and it sounds as though they're about to be invaded. The question is, what will we do about it?' Arthur's face was grim.

He finished speaking, and Margaret's stomach churned as she and her husband exchanged glances and the significance of the news for their family — especially their son — sank in.

2

As she lifted the cover from the type-writer in her office, Margaret realised she didn't remember anything of her journey into work.

One thing she could remember was the way she'd somehow got herself back together for her daughter's sake after the shock of hearing the news about the Falkland Islands.

'It's been a long week,' she'd told her worried daughter, Alison, while her husband, joining in the charade, had yawned and stretched as if in agreement. 'Pick up your PE socks from the airing cupboard and get yourself off to school.'

At the office, there was something reassuring about the old building with its solid walls and her trusty typewriter, waiting for her as always.

Even the handrail on the mahogany banisters was worn smooth from countless hands, Margaret reflected as she made her way back downstairs to collect Mr Clarence's post.

She paused when she saw that almost everyone was still in reception, lingering longer than they usually did for exchanging morning pleasantries.

Young Paul, one of the solicitors, was leaning on the desk. He often did that, always ready for a chat that had a way of putting everyone in a lighter mood.

Today, though, they all seemed subdued.

Pam, the receptionist, and Karen, the junior secretary, barely said hello as they sorted the post into wire baskets. Helen, the new girl, stood to one side, as if she'd like to join in but hadn't yet found her feet.

Paul turned round and saw Margaret first.

'How are you doing, Margaret?' He placed one hand on her shoulder. 'Everyone's heard the news. It doesn't exactly put you in a Friday mood, does it?

'Still, things will be sorted out soon

and we can all go back to complaining about the weather.'

The others nodded.

Mr Clarence's office door opened and a hush descended as the senior partner stepped out.

He frowned.

'Margaret?'

'I'm about to bring your post through, Mr Clarence.'

'Very well.'

When he consulted his watch, everyone took the hint and went their separate ways.

A couple of minutes later, Margaret placed the correspondence tray on Mr Clarence's desk, as she took pride in doing every morning without fail.

Instead of acknowledging receipt and carrying on with his work, her boss looked intently at her.

'You're pale, Margaret.'

'It's been a busy couple of weeks, Mr Clarence. None of us is at our best.'

'You can't pull the wool over my eyes. I listen to the news, too, you know.'

Margaret sighed.

'As does the whole office, apparently. I'm all for being close-knit, but it would be nice to have some privacy.'

'It has its advantages at times. I'm sure the matter will be resolved, but I can understand your concern for Adam.

'Every family with someone in the Armed Forces will be worried today.' He leaned forward. 'I hope you don't mind my speaking as your friend as well as your employer.'

Margaret felt her cheeks grow warm. For goodness' sake, the last time she'd blushed in his presence she'd been about twenty-two.

'If there's anything you want — even if you just need to talk — my door is open.'

'Thank you, Mr Clarence.'

Her boss inclined his head.

'Look, why don't you go home? We'll manage without you.'

Margaret squared her shoulders.

'I'll stay, if you don't mind. Fridays are busy, and I find that work is the best distraction from other matters.'

Her colleague of all these years sat back in his chair.

'I know what you mean,' Mr Clarence replied. 'Promise me that if you find it all getting too much, you'll go home and rest.'

Within minutes, Margaret was back in her own office, settling down to some typing. The rhythmic tapping of the keys and speed of her fingers soothed her, as did the murmur and pulse of office life in the background.

She had just finished a letter regarding a contested right of way when she was aware of someone tapping at the door and looked round to see Helen standing nervously in the doorway.

'I'm sorry about the news this morning,' the girl said. 'If there's anything I can do, I'm more than willing to help. I'm a dab hand with the photocopier, for instance.'

Margaret felt her eyes prick with tears. She blinked them away.

'Thank you, Helen. Don't be offended

if I turn down your offer. It is appreciated, though.' She hesitated before adding, 'I'm not sure if I've said it before, but I hope you'll be happy here.'

She meant it, too, she realised. She may have had her views on a slip of a girl being a solicitor, but it was time to overcome such attitudes, along with her fears for Adam.

★ ★ ★

That evening, Helen stepped off the bus with a sigh of relief. She couldn't remember when she had last felt so exhausted.

Birds were singing in the trees lining the road as if to celebrate the lengthening daylight hours, as well as to mark the end of another day.

Already, after living there for a week, small landmarks were becoming familiar to her. There was the beech hedge at the front of Number Five, for instance, and the bird bath in the garden of Number Nine, where a black cat also watched eagerly from the window.

Further along, a woman and an older man were unloading boxes from a car and carrying them into one of the other houses.

There was something about the way the woman moved that rang a bell.

With cars being parked all along the road, it was only when she'd almost reached her own house that she realised where the boxes were being taken. The realisation was confirmed when she saw Jackie at the front door.

'The new tenant's here,' she announced. 'She seems nice. Her name is — '

'Helen?'

Helen jumped at the sound of a familiar voice behind her. She turned round, pasting on a smile.

'Hello, Diane. What are the odds of us both moving into the same house?'

'About a hundred to one, I should think. What brings you to this neck of the woods?'

'A new job. I, er, felt it was time to move on.'

Diane, her eyes as dark brown and face as grave as ever, nodded slowly.

'Yes, I can imagine how you would.'

Helen was spared from saying more as Jackie joined the conversation.

'You know each other?'

Helen and Diane exchanged a glance before Diane stepped back slightly, as if to give Helen room to tell as much as she decided.

'Yes, we went to the same university. We were on different courses, but we had several mutual friends, so we saw each other a lot.'

'And now you're back together!' Jackie exclaimed, breaking the awkward silence that fell between them. 'Talk about landing on our feet. I'll get the kettle on, then we can get to know each other and marvel at what a small world it is.'

She rolled her eyes as the phone in the hall started ringing.

'That'll be my mum. She said she'd call this evening. See you in a minute.'

Once Helen and Diane were left

alone, Diane was the first to speak.

'Have you heard from Tony lately?'

Helen swallowed.

'No. Have you?'

'A bit.'

Even though nearly four years had passed since they'd left university, Helen wasn't surprised Diane and Tony were still in touch. The two had been close friends.

She lifted her chin.

'How is he?'

'Much as you'd expect in the circumstances.' Diane shifted her gaze to a point somewhere across the road. 'Helen — '

She was interrupted as the older man came out of the house.

'We're about done now. Jackie's putting the kettle on, so after I've had a cuppa I'll leave you to it.'

'Thanks, Dad.' Diane hugged him. 'You've been brilliant. I don't know what I'd do without you.'

Helen wasn't sure whether to be relieved that the conversation had been ended or not. Probably the former, though it was almost certainly only postponing the inevitable.

She'd moved here to get away from the past, but it seemed the past was determined to follow her.

Luckily Diane was too busy getting settled into her new room to talk much that first evening. In fact, all three of them, worn out from a busy few days, were happy to settle for an early night.

*   *   *

Helen managed to avoid both of her housemates the next morning, luxuriating in a Saturday lie-in and waiting till the sound of their chatter in the kitchen had died away before she ventured downstairs.

She achieved further avoidance by embarking on the trip to town she'd promised herself.

When she got there she was surprised by how busy the centre was, as well as the range of stores in what some would regard as a backwater.

Technically it must be a city, she supposed, walking past the front of the cathedral. It felt far more comfortable than most cities she'd ever been in.

She crossed the road to the shopping centre and was tempted to look in the window of an impressive jeweller's adjacent to the entrance, when she came to an abrupt stop. Wasn't that Karen going in with a good-looking young man?

Something told her there could be some interesting news at the office come Monday.

Karen hadn't seen her, so she continued on, passing a bakery and a bookshop in favour of a selection of clothes shops mixing high street chains and lesser-known names.

She was just about to make for one of her favourite chains when she spotted Margaret with a shy-looking teenage girl, presumably her daughter.

For the second time that morning, Helen changed direction. Was there no escape, either from work or the past?

Perhaps a browse in the bookshop

would provide some light relief. She certainly needed it.

★ ★ ★

What was it about fifteen-year-olds that made them so awkward, Margaret wondered as Alison led her into another clothes shop.

Her daughter kept picking up a dress here, a top there, and dismissing everything apart from the garments Margaret regarded as too expensive or impractical. Her own mother would never have let her get away with such choices.

Still, it was nice to go shopping together. They hadn't done this for a while, now that Alison was at the age where she was more argumentative about what she should wear, as well as awkward about being seen out in public with her mother.

Clearly it had reached the point where necessity outweighed embarrassment, but Margaret wasn't complaining.

'How about this puffball dress, Mum?

I love turquoise, and the style's really in at the moment.'

Alison held out the dress on its hanger.

Although Margaret had seen puffball dresses in the fashion pages of the Sunday supplements, she hadn't noticed anyone wearing them in real life. The skirt bulged out and went round under itself rather than ending in a normal hem as most dresses did.

Goodness only knew how they were supposed to be ironed, or how they kept their shape after the wearer had sat down in one. For all that, she had to admit it looked interesting, and it was only natural that Alison would want something fashionable.

'The colour brings out the blue of your eyes, and the bodice does go in nicely at the waist,' she agreed, trying not to flinch at the price tag. 'I've heard the style is a difficult one to pull off, though. It all depends on whether the skirt hangs right on you.'

'Can I try it on, Mum?'

Margaret faltered.

'It isn't exactly an everyday dress. When would you wear it?'

'At my sixteenth birthday party. That's less than two months away, you know. If it's anywhere near as big as Adam's was, I'll need something special.'

'Go on. I'm not making any promises, mind.'

As she waited for her daughter outside the fitting-room, Margaret crossed her fingers that Adam would be at the party.

The shadow of events in the southern Atlantic made her shiver, even in the warmth of a shopping centre that was full of bustle and chatter.

Ten minutes later, her bank account was significantly lighter, while Alison proudly carried a bag emblazoned with the shop's logo.

'Thank you so much, Mum.' Her eyes sparkled as they sat down together to enjoy toasted teacakes, oozing with melting butter, and a hot drink in their favourite café on the balcony overlooking the market.

'That's going to be a dress I'll love for ages.'

Assuming it wasn't going to be out of fashion by the following year, Margaret thought, but knew better than to say out loud.

'It looks good on you. It will be perfect for your sixteenth. We'll have to start making plans for that in a few weeks.'

Alison seemed to concentrate intently on stirring her hot chocolate.

'Do you think Adam will make it?' she asked, as if picking up on Margaret's earlier worries.

'That depends on if he can get leave. I'm sure he'll move heaven and earth to be with his little sister.'

'What if there's a war?'

Margaret's fingers tightened round the handle of her coffee mug.

'What makes you think there will be?' she asked airily.

'Well, there was the news on the radio yesterday.'

'Oh, that'll be sorted out, somehow or other.' Margaret tried to sound confident and remember the points Mr Clarence had made.

'Most countries will do anything to avoid going to war. By the time it's your birthday we'll be shaking our heads and wondering what the fuss was about.'

'But what if there is?' Alison persisted. 'Everyone at school thinks there will be. Some people in my class know that Adam's in the Army, and they kept saying he'll have to fight.'

Margaret shook her head.

'Then they're not very nice individuals and are doing it only to upset you. You have to learn not to take notice of people like them.' She softened her tone.

'What will be will be. If things happen, we deal with them, as we always have. That's what life's about.

'Now, I could do with some new shoes for work, so finish your cake and help me choose some,' Margaret added.

By the time they'd finished, both weighed down with several bags, the newspaper vendors were taking up their posts around the town, with their cries of ''Evening Telegraph'!'

For Margaret, in town virtually every day, they were part of the scenery, so she barely gave more than a glance at the headlines on the boards beside them.

Today, though, she felt drawn to look, and what she saw made her go cold inside.

Falklands Task Force Announced!

She hurried Alison along on the pretext that they needed to rush to catch the bus, in the hope that her daughter wouldn't read it, and all the time trying to ignore the pounding of her heart.

⋆   ⋆   ⋆

Clarence had thought that Eleanor was going to take their teenage daughter to her riding lesson on Saturday afternoon, but his wife had ended up visiting a friend who was having a family problem, so the job fell to him.

Part of him suspected this was a plot to get him away from his desk, yet he

48

couldn't help a surge of paternal pride as he saw Samantha in the jodhpurs and riding boots she'd asked for last Christmas, rather than make-up or other items he assumed girls of her age preferred.

Her riding hat had been a Christmas present from her grandmother.

Clarence felt a lump in his throat as he imagined how she would have loved seeing Sam looking so smart today.

A sweater and anorak completed the outfit, and he had the sense that nothing would have suited her better.

'I hope I'm riding Charlie today,' Sam said as they arrived at the stables. 'He's my favourite. I've brought him some mints.'

By the time he'd paid Vanessa, the proprietor, his daughter was already on the friendly-looking grey pony and was adjusting her stirrups. He squeezed her hand and gave Charlie a friendly pat.

'Have a good time. I'll see you in an hour.'

It hardly seemed worth going home. Once he'd settled down to work it would be time to set out again.

Instead, Clarence turned his car in the opposite direction; up on to the moors, pulling into a rough parking area that was popular with walkers as a setting-off point, or just for taking in the view.

The silence enveloped him within seconds of switching off the engine.

It briefly occurred to him that this would have been the perfect place to work without any interruptions. The notion even made him slightly fidgety at first, before the sheer sense of space worked its magic and he gave himself up to it.

Zipping up his jacket, he climbed out of the car and walked over to an outcrop giving an unparalleled panorama of the valley.

All around, the wild moorland grasses had been bleached and scoured by the cold winds of winter. The effect was desolate and bleak, yet beautiful.

Cradled at the bottom of the valley lay the old mill town he'd known all his life. It might not be glamorous or pretty, but it was home. He couldn't imagine ever wanting to leave.

His son, Peter, and his brother, James, had both left, though, tearing rifts in the family in the process.

James could have come back from Australia at any time and faced up to his responsibilities, but he'd chosen to stay away, only turning up for their mother's funeral last week.

Now it seemed Peter was heading down the same route. Clarence hadn't spoken to his son in five years.

Up here, Eleanor's comments about the dangers of history repeating itself resonated more deeply. Yet family continuity and traditions mattered. His father had worked hard, building up the business, and it was up to other generations to preserve his legacy, but James and Peter both had chosen different paths.

A chill wind made him turn up his collar. It was almost time to collect Sam, though doubtless she'd be happily making a fuss of Charlie.

Clarence wasn't prepared, then, for the sight that greeted him when he got to the stables.

Vanessa was waiting for him in the yard with a very pale-looking Samantha. His stomach clenched as he noticed his daughter was holding her arm awkwardly.

'What's happened?' he asked.

'She fell off when something spooked her horse,' Vanessa replied. 'There was nothing anyone could do about it.'

'My wrist hurts, Dad.' Sam indicated her left arm, which he could see now was swollen. Someone had given her a bag of frozen peas to hold against it.

Clarence's business-like side took over. 'Let's go to the hospital.'

★   ★   ★

The Casualty department at the infirmary was busy but not frantically so, and staff assured Clarence and Sam that the wait shouldn't be long.

'I'm sorry, Dad,' Sam said when they'd found a couple of free chairs.

'Whatever for?'

'I fell off Charlie. I should have been in control of him. I feel like I've failed.'

Clarence ruffled her hair to cover his shock at her stricken expression.

'Accidents happen,' he told her with a smile. 'You wouldn't believe the number of times your gran used to bring Uncle James here. He was always falling off his bike or out of trees.'

'Peter, too,' Sam pointed out with a giggle. 'Remember that time he was trying to build me a treehouse, reached too far and the branch wouldn't hold his weight?'

'Not in detail. I was busy in court. His arm was already in plaster by the time I saw him.'

'And everyone wrote on it.' Sam giggled again. 'I miss him. Do you think he'll come home soon?'

Clarence was saved from having to answer by a nurse calling them through.

Thankfully, Samantha had suffered nothing worse than a badly sprained wrist, though it meant riding would be out of the question for a while.

'Maybe it's just as well,' was her reaction as they drove home. 'I need to work harder to get good marks in my exams.'

She paused.

'When I was waiting with Vanessa, she was worried you might sue her. You won't, will you?'

Clarence frowned.

'Of course not. Some of my clients can be somewhat litigious, but that doesn't mean I am. There's no need to worry. The real fun's going to be explaining all this to your mother.'

★ ★ ★

Safely home, Clarence phoned the stables' proprietor to update her. Her nervousness came across loud and clear, and he put the receiver down with a heavy heart. Everyone seemed to be so defensive around him nowadays.

'Sam,' he began as he walked into the living-room. 'Do I come across as some sort of an ogre?'

She glanced up from watching television.

'Well, you can be a bit strict sometimes.'

Before he could press her further, she'd turned her attention back to the programme, signalling that the conversation was over.

* * *

The coast seemed clear as Helen staggered in with two bulging carrier bags of shopping, containing enough provisions to keep her going for a while.

She'd just put away the last tin of beans when the sound of someone clearing their throat made her look round to see Diane in the doorway, looking almost as uncomfortable as Helen felt.

'I was just coming down to get a coffee. I can go away until you've finished in here, if you like.'

'No, it's OK. Go ahead.'

'Shall I put some water in for you? You could probably do with a cuppa if you've been busy.'

Helen's instinct was to get to her room as quickly as possible, but she gave herself a shake. She could hardly keep avoiding the inevitable.

'That would be nice. How are you settling in?' It seemed rude not to ask.

'It's getting there. My room is almost sorted, and I'm OK for food. Mum packed a box-load for me.' Diane rolled her eyes.

'Why did you leave home? You come from this area, don't you?'

'It's less of a journey to work. I work in a bank in town and my parents live out in the country.

'Plus it's awkward living with your parents when you're twenty-five, so it was time to make the move.' She spooned coffee into two mugs. 'Sugar?'

'One, please, and milk. Thanks.'

Diane looked thoughtful.

'I hope you don't think I'm speaking out of turn, but I know about you and Tony. He was one of my best friends at university and he's a great bloke, but I know how wilful he can be at times.

'Don't blame yourself for what happened. It was just rotten luck. Let's start with a clean sheet, eh?'

Helen sagged with relief.

'Thank you for being understanding. I hope you know that wasn't why I — '

She stopped as the front door opened. A minute later, Jackie joined them.

'Oh, has the kettle just boiled? I could murder a hot drink.'

Soon the three of them were sitting round the table.

'It's so good to have housemates I can have a natter with,' Jackie said, dunking a bourbon cream in her coffee. 'Why don't we have a girls' night out this evening? I reckon we deserve it.'

Helen and Diane glanced at each other.

'Yes, why not?' Diane said as they all clinked mugs in agreement.

★   ★   ★

The atmosphere in the nightclub a few hours later was friendly. Everyone seemed intent on a carefree night out after a long week at work.

As they danced to old favourites mixed

up with the latest chart hits, Helen felt the tensions of the past few days start to slip away.

Jackie was invited to dance by a cheerful-looking man, while, minutes later, Diane was dancing with a tall, lanky lad who could probably grin for England.

Feeling awkward, Helen went to sit down, when one of her favourite David Bowie tracks came on.

As she tapped her foot, nearly dancing on the spot, a dark-haired man with smiling eyes approached.

'Would you like to dance?' he asked, almost shouting to be heard above the music.

Helen smiled and nodded.

When the song ended, they both stood awkwardly, unsure of what to do next, until the unmistakable guitar riff from 'Brown Sugar' blared out and his face lit up.

'I love this!'

'So do I,' she agreed.

'I'm happy to keep dancing if you are.'

After a few more songs, all six of them gathered at the same table, happily getting along as a group.

'I didn't get a chance to introduce myself before,' Helen's dancing partner said. 'I'm Peter, and I'm pleased to meet you.'

With their general chatter, interspersed with more dancing, it soon felt as though they had all been friends for months rather than a few short hours.

Helen couldn't remember when she'd last enjoyed herself so much, much less believe it when the DJ announced the last song of the evening and the dance floor filled once more.

All too soon the music faded.

Peter smiled as their eyes met.

'It's been a fantastic evening. I hadn't expected to have such a good time.'

'Same here,' Helen replied.

She wasn't sure how they came to be in each other's arms, but it felt like the most natural thing in the world, as did the kiss they shared, only drawing apart when the lights came up and made everyone blink.

'Can I see you again?' Peter asked.

Helen nodded.

'When would suit you?' he went on. 'I'm busy this weekend, but I could call you next week, if you like?'

It was only when she was in her room later that she realised she hadn't thought of Tony all evening. She'd been enjoying herself, while he was stuck in a wheelchair. What sort of person did that make her?

Still, she returned to work on Monday refreshed and ready to take on another week, so was curious rather than apprehensive when Mr Clarence called her into his office.

'I wanted to ask you about that accident compensation claim we took on. Do you remember I pointed out it was coming up to the third anniversary, so a High Court Writ needed to be issued?'

Helen was aware that if court proceedings weren't started within three years of the date of an accident, the claim could be barred.

'I've just checked in the diary. The

writ has to be issued by today, but there's no mention of it. Did you omit to record it?'

Helen's heart plummeted. She'd drafted the writ on Friday, meaning to take it to the local court in person, but that morning's news meant she'd forgotten.

Her face must have given away her guilt. When the senior partner spoke again, his measured tone somehow made things worse.

'I strongly advise you to go and do it now. I must say I am more than a little concerned. If I hadn't checked, the deadline could have been missed, prejudicing our client's interests and laying the firm open to a suit for negligence. We'll discuss the ramifications for your employment here later.'

It was only when Helen came out of the court office, the writ safely issued, that she felt able to breathe again, but not for long, because the fact remained that she had made a basic and potentially disastrous mistake — one that could even have cost her her job.

3

After Helen had left his office, Clarence shuffled some papers distractedly for a few minutes, before a knock at the door heralded Margaret striding in with an expression on her face he'd seen on various occasions when she'd given a member of staff a ticking off.

He wondered who was in trouble this time.

'I don't have any dictation for you at the moment, Margaret.'

'That's not what I'm here for, Mr Clarence.'

'Really?' He gestured to a seat on the far side of the desk, but his secretary remained standing.

'I couldn't help overhearing what happened just now. Nor could half of reception, thanks to the door not being shut properly. I came to close it and heard the last part of the conversation.'

Margaret cleared her throat. 'Does Miss Martin really deserve to be sacked?'

'Do you make a habit of eavesdropping?' The words were out of his mouth before he realised what he was saying.

Margaret's eyes widened.

'After working together for over twenty-five years, you know very well I don't.'

'Sorry.' Clarence held up his hands. 'My remark was uncalled for. However, presumably you heard enough to know she made a potentially serious error, which could have caused a lot of problems and damaged our reputation.

'That's important, Margaret. Clients come to us because they trust us to do a good job.'

Margaret nodded.

'Absolutely, and you had to point it out in no uncertain terms,' she agreed, 'but was it necessary to be so hard on someone who's new here and still finding their feet?

'You weren't perfect when you started out, as I recall. You had a few dressings down from your father, but he never threatened you with the sack.'

'You're right. Consider me well and truly told off. I'll straighten things out with Helen, though I'm in court this morning and have clients for the rest of the day.' He let out a long breath.

'I don't know what I'd do without you to keep me on the right path, Margaret. I can only blame my bad temper on recent events.'

Immediately, he could have kicked himself. His own setbacks paled in comparison with hers.

'More importantly, how are you? Any news from Adam?' he asked her.

This time Margaret took the seat she'd been offered.

'Some.' She glanced at Clarence. 'I take it you've heard about the task force that's setting off for the Falklands? Adam's regiment is included.' Her voice shook on the last few words.

Clarence shook his head.

'I'm sorry. It must have been a difficult weekend for you all.'

'I can't pretend it's been easy. Alison was asking questions. We had a heart to heart. She's suggested we postpone her sixteenth birthday party, but we persuaded her that her brother would feel bad if she did because of him.'

She swallowed.

'I wonder how many families are going through the same,' she continued. 'Whatever the rights and wrongs of the matter, it's ordinary folk who are caught up in the middle of it all.' She stood up.

'But it's also ordinary folk who have to keep the wheels turning.'

'Are you sure you're not pushing yourself too hard in order to keep everything else at bay? Maybe you should ease up,' Clarence suggested kindly.

Margaret snorted.

'How many times have people told you the same thing? And since when have you taken their advice on that or on other matters?'

★   ★   ★

Clarence was in pensive mood as he walked through town to the local county court. He'd known what Margaret had been referring to about his working too hard and other matters, and remembered Samantha's comments on Saturday.

When she'd been told she wouldn't be able to ride for a while, she'd joked that she needed the extra time to study for her exams. Was she starting to feel the same pressures he had?

The hearing, an application for a court order to evict squatters from his client's property, was to be held in open court before a judge, requiring a full formal robe.

In the solicitors' robing room, two other solicitors he vaguely knew were there, laughing unpleasantly.

'You should have seen her,' one of them said. 'You'd think she'd never issued a writ in her life. It's a mistake letting all these young women into the profession. They only go off and get married anyway. I'd never employ one.'

He looked slyly round at Clarence,

who felt his hackies rise.

'Presumably you're both aware of the Sex Discrimination Act?' he asked coolly.

'Oh, come on,' the other solicitor replied. 'We can speak our minds. We're all men here.'

Clarence didn't get the chance to say anything further, as the court usher entered the room at that moment.

'Make your way through, please. The judge is ready.'

★   ★   ★

Once she'd returned from the court, with the writ safely issued, the need for action that had kept Helen going so far dissolved.

She had taken sanctuary in her office when Karen popped her head round the door.

'Are you OK?'

Helen slumped back in her chair.

'I suppose everyone knows what happened?'

Karen nodded.

'Don't worry. As I said last week, everyone's nice here. Mrs Hall went in to see Mr Clarence. I think she told him off, because he seemed a bit quieter when he set off for court a few minutes ago. You must have just missed him.'

'That's the first good thing that's happened to me all morning. I can't believe I made such a big mistake.' Helen sighed.

'Well, there was plenty going on to distract you. I've been struggling to concentrate, too.' Karen hesitated. 'If I tell you something, can you keep it to yourself?'

'Of course. Am I the best person, though?'

'You're the nearest in age to me.' Karen pulled up a chair. 'I was in town with my boyfriend on Saturday, and we ended up looking at engagement rings. He hasn't proposed yet, but he hinted that he's been saving up. There were some lovely ones and I was really tempted, but I'm not sure I want to get engaged.'

Helen blew out her cheeks.

'Do you love him?'

'I think so. When Prince Charles said, 'Whatever love is', when he and Lady Diana got engaged, it seemed a bit strange, yet I sort of know what he meant.'

'Oh.' Helen frowned. 'Maybe you should think carefully about it before you get in too deep.'

'But I don't want to disappoint him.'

'Sometimes you don't have a choice.'

Karen looked steadily at her for a moment, and seemed to be on the point of asking more, when the phone rang.

'I've got a new client for you,' Pam, the receptionist, said. 'A lady tripped over an uneven paving slab and ended up with a broken wrist. Can you see her?'

★ ★ ★

That evening, Helen and Diane chatted in the kitchen as they sorted out something to eat.

'I'm sure everything will be fine,' was

Diane's reaction when Helen told her what had happened. 'You got a timely shake-up, that's all. It's often a rocky road when you start a new job. At least your social life's looking good.'

She nudged her.

'You seemed to be getting along nicely with Peter on Saturday night.'

'But I even felt bad about that afterwards,' Helen confessed.

'Because of Tony? You can't punish yourself for ever. You have to move on. Will you see Peter again?'

'Possibly, I've given him our number. I'm not sure if I'm ready to start seeing someone new, to be honest. Maybe he won't call and it won't arise.'

As if to prove her wrong, the phone rang at that moment, echoing from the hall and making her jump.

On answering, the sound of pips indicated someone was calling from a phone box, followed by the sound of Peter's voice.

'Helen? How are you? Do you like Clint Eastwood? One of his 'Dirty

Harry' films is showing at the cinema this evening and I was wondering if you'd like to see it with me.'

Helen suddenly felt about six inches taller.

'I love Clint Eastwood, and I could do with an evening out,' she replied.

'Great. I'll pick you up in about an hour. We can go for a drink afterwards if it isn't too late by then.'

Helen just had time to make an omelette and change into jeans and an embroidered top before the doorbell rang.

As she opened the door, her heart skipped a beat at the sight of Peter's smile. He was just as attractive as she remembered.

When they got to the pavement and he stopped by a parked car, though, the skip turned to a thud.

'Can we walk? The cinema's only down the road. You might as well save the petrol.'

Peter chuckled.

'Thanks for the thought, but we're not going to that one. The film's on at the other side of town.' He unlocked the passenger door and held it open for her. 'Hop in.'

Over the next few minutes, Helen's nails dug into her hands as she tried to quell her panic.

She couldn't help squeaking: 'Mind that car' and 'Slow down' at regular intervals.

'Don't worry,' Peter told her. 'I grew up around here. I even had a spell of driving taxis for a living.'

He slowed down, even though he'd already been safely within the speed limit.

'Are you OK?' he asked once they'd parked. 'You look peaky. Are you sure you're up to seeing the film?'

'Not really,' Helen admitted. 'Do you mind?'

'Of course not. We can see it another night. Let's go for a drink. There's a nice pub near here.'

Once they'd found a seat by the fire, Peter brought over a glass of lager for Helen and a soft drink for himself. He gazed searchingly into her eyes.

'I might have only recently met you, but I can tell this is more than a case of feeling a bit off colour. Do you want to talk about it?'

'You'll think it's ridiculous,' Helen warned.

'Try me.'

She took a deep breath.

'I had a bad experience in a car crash months ago.'

'Does that mean you can't travel in a car?'

'No, but I do need some warning. I should have realised we'd be in a car this evening. I'm so sorry.' She took a gulp of her lager and nodded at the TV near the bar where news reports showed destroyers heading off for the Falkland Islands.

'It's crazy, isn't it? All those soldiers heading thousands of miles away from home, while I'm a nervous wreck from riding in a car.'

'We're all scared of something,' Peter told her. 'I'm hardly perfect myself.'

If only you knew, Helen thought.

Margaret checked off dates on her calendar.

'Today is the fifth of April,' she told her daughter. 'Your birthday is the twenty-eighth of May, so we'll have the party the day after. That's seven weeks on Saturday.' She wrote Alison's name against the date.

'You'll be surprised how quickly the time passes.'

She flipped the calendar back to April and hung it on its hook.

'I'll make a list of people to invite later in the week. I'm too tired to do anything tonight as it's been a busy day, but at least we know what to plan towards.'

'It feels wrong having the party without Adam being here.' Alison put some of her schoolbooks down on the dining table.

She often did homework there rather than in her room, saying it was warmer and she liked being able to chat. Margaret suspected the table's proximity to the kitchen, complete with snacks, also had something to do with it.

'What did we agree when we talked about it on Saturday?' she reminded her daughter. 'He'd hate you to put it off.

'We can have another party when he gets back — in the summer holidays. Your exams will be out of the way by then, too.'

Alison's shoulders sagged.

'My birthday party will be right in the middle of the exams.'

'It will also be during the bank holiday weekend and at the start of half term, when you'll have time to relax as well as revise.

'You can't revise all the time,' Margaret pointed out. 'You're a bright girl. If you do well in your exams, that will set you up for the future.'

Her words didn't have the motivating effect she'd hoped for and Alison's eyes filled with tears.

'I'm not sure I can cope, Mum. I can't stop worrying about Adam on the one hand, and exams on the other.'

'Oh, love.' Margaret hugged her. 'Try to look at the exams as a way to keep your mind occupied. I often find work helps me lose myself, though I know that isn't the same for everyone.

'If you find it difficult to concentrate, do something you enjoy to get yourself into the flow. Things will work out.'

Alison wiped her eyes.

'Thanks, Mum. I'll do that and make Adam proud. He's always liked teasing me for being a swot. And I'll have that birthday party. I'll wear that dress we bought on Saturday.'

'That's the spirit. Once that's done, we can start planning for Adam's party.'

She hoped Alison couldn't see her crossing her fingers behind her back.

Monday night was spaghetti bolognese night in the Hall household, cooked by her husband Arthur, who boasted that he made the best spag bol this side of Italy.

Shortly after he got home and they'd exchanged their day's happenings, Alison popped up to her room, leaving her parents alone in the kitchen. Margaret

76

took advantage of her absence to tell her husband about their daughter's worries.

'I hope I gave her good advice,' she said as she passed a tin of tomatoes from the cupboard.

'I'm sure you did. You've always had a common-sense approach that has stood us in good stead.' He chuckled. 'Even at our wedding you made sure that what was left of the wedding cake was put straight into tins to keep it fresh for longer.'

'I should think so, too, after all the hard work my mother put in to making it,' Margaret retorted.

'And it was worth it,' Arthur agreed. 'That cake kept us going for weeks afterwards, which was useful, bearing in mind we hardly had enough money for basic groceries, never mind treats.'

'I don't suppose Adam is getting much in the way of treats at the moment.' Margaret stared out of the window. 'I wonder how far the task force has got.'

'Not far if they sailed today. It's a long voyage.'

'In the southern hemisphere, the seasons will be the other way round. It must be autumn there.'

She went over to the bookshelves and picked out the world atlas, which had been used more in the last few days than it had for years.

She wasn't sure whether following Adam's progress on a map made her feel closer to him, or made things harder because it was so real.

'Whatever season it is, and whatever happens, I'm proud of you,' Arthur said. 'Look at how much you always manage to do.'

'You're no slacker yourself,' Margaret teased. 'People at work have been helpful, so I can't take all the credit. Mr Clarence has been very understanding, and Karen has been a revelation.

'She's been taking on more typing to help out and is enjoying the extra responsibility. She reminds me of my younger self. It made me smile today.'

'What? You mean instead of breathing fire, like your usual dragon self?'

Margaret was laughing as she opened the atlas and found the relevant page.

Her laughter faded as she looked properly at the map and realised how far her son had to sail on the cold Atlantic, not knowing what might be waiting for him at the end of the voyage.

★   ★   ★

Helen and Peter went out several times over the next few weeks. They kept to destinations within walking distance of her house or caught a bus into the town centre, where he joked that at least he wouldn't have to worry about parking his car.

Conversation came easily to them, chatting about everything apart from work, and the reason she was so nervous of travelling in a car.

Although she trusted Peter instinctively, she was still reluctant to open up about her past, worried that once he knew the reason she would almost certainly lose him.

Tulips shed their petals as April slipped into May and spring strengthened its tentative hold. Evenings stayed lighter for longer, occasionally warm enough for them to sit outside with their drinks in the beer garden of what had become their favoured pub.

Wallflowers bloomed in the borders while birds hopped about, digging in the grass for worms to carry back to broods in their nests.

'Some swallows are back,' Peter commented. 'I've seen them nesting at the farm where I've been working.'

'How's the renovation work at your friend's house coming on?' Helen asked. He was renting a room there cheaply in exchange for help to do it up.

'It's getting there now winter's out-of the way, but there's a long way to go. It was completely dilapidated when he took it on.

'You must see it once it's finished. Do you think you'll be ready by then?'

The house and farm were both in the next town, which would mean travelling in the car.

'Maybe.' Helen leaned back and stretched her arms. 'Isn't it nice to see everything coming back to life? I can feel my energy increasing with every day.'

Peter raised his eyebrows at the change of subject.

'Is your confidence increasing, too?'

'At work? Yes, I think I'm getting used to it.'

'Do you happen to know a firm with . . . ' Peter began, but stopped.

He'd done the same thing a couple of times, giving Helen the impression she wasn't the only one holding something back.

'What?'

He shook his head.

'Nothing important. Enough about work. We've always agreed our time together is for relaxing. You're only using it to evade the real question.'

'You're right.' Helen sighed. 'I'm going to have to do something about this car phobia. I passed my driving test a couple of years ago, but I haven't driven much since then because of the expense of buying and running a car.'

Peter reached across and put his hand over hers.

'I haven't pressed you on the matter because I didn't feel it was my place, but don't you think we know each other well enough by now for you to be able to tell me what this is about?

'You've already told me that you were in car crash, but so are lots of people, yet they're able to put it behind them. There's something deeper upsetting you, isn't there?'

Helen twisted her glass round.

'If I tell you, you'll think I'm a horrible person.'

'You don't know that. I'm no saint myself. A bit of a black sheep, in fact. I'm a major disappointment to my family. Well, most of them.' He shrugged.

'Why? What happened?'

'I told my parents I didn't want to follow the path they'd planned for me.

Mum wasn't too bad about it, but my dad was livid.

'We had a blazing row and he more or less said that if I walked out the door I shouldn't come back.'

Helen frowned.

'That sounds harsh. Are you sure he meant it?'

Peter's mouth set in a grim line.

'Yes. I walked out and haven't gone back since. Looking back, I wish I'd done things differently. I've travelled around, doing odd jobs here and there to make ends meet, never settling anywhere and never wanting to. Until now.' He gazed at her.

'So, you see, you're going out with a good-for-nothing drifter.'

It was Helen's turn to reach for Peter's hand.

'No way are you good for nothing. You're intelligent, kind and resourceful. Nor are you a drifter. You want to go to agricultural college.'

'You're making me blush.' His expression turned serious again. 'See? You know about me, and you don't mind, because you're the sort of person who sees past the surface. Let me do the same for you.'

Helen took a long drink of her lager.

'OK. I was going out with a guy called Tony. We were at uni together and carried on seeing each other afterwards. We got engaged.' She smiled sadly. 'Then things changed.

'I started wondering if that was what I really wanted. Then there was the accident. He was driving too fast, and we were involved in a crash.

'I got away with a broken arm and a few minor injuries, but Tony was in hospital for months.'

'That's bad,' Peter sympathised. 'But I don't see why it's left you with such a psychological scar.'

'Because that's not all.' Helen gulped down the rest of her drink. 'Tony didn't just end up in hospital. He ended up in a wheelchair, where he'll be for the rest of his life.

'It was my fault he was driving too

fast. I'd just broken up with him.

'Afterwards, I could see the accusation in everyone's eyes, even if they didn't actually say anything.

'I did the only thing I could think of and found another job and moved away to make a fresh start.'

She held her breath as Peter, jaw set, pushed away his glass. Though only a few seconds passed, it seemed an age before he spoke.

'It looks as if we're both exiles. I'm glad we found each other.'

Helen felt her heart swell at his words.

'So am I,' she agreed.

★ ★ ★

'How long does it take to get that thing going?' someone joked as Arthur blew on the charcoals to try to bring the barbecue to life. 'We'll die of starvation at this rate.'

Luckily, everything else was going smoothly at Alison's party. Margaret had prepared plenty of sausage rolls, vol-au-vents and a big bowl of salad, so that no-one went hungry.

If anything, the barbecue's reluctance to co-operate worked in her favour, giving her time to butter a mountain of rolls.

They'd been lucky with the weather. Everyone mingled comfortably in the garden, sitting on a mixed collection of chairs and benches.

Younger guests settled on rugs under the apple tree, amusingly enchanted by pink blossom drifting down and landing in their hair.

Margaret was emptying bags of crisps into bowls when Eleanor Barnes came into the kitchen.

'Would you like a hand? It seems wrong to let you do all the work while everyone else is enjoying themselves.'

Margaret hurriedly straightened her dress to look more presentable for her boss's wife.

'That's all right, Mrs Barnes. Everything's pretty much organised. Can I get you a drink? There's some white wine in the fridge, or I could put the kettle on if you'd prefer a cup of tea.'

'Please, call me Eleanor. Perhaps I can prepare some more salad? It seems to be going down quickly, thanks to the weather.'

'Thank you.' Thank goodness she'd cleared the fridge out earlier in the week, ready for all the extra food.

'It's going well, isn't it?' Eleanor started slicing cucumber on a chopping board. 'Alison looks as pretty as a picture. We were chatting just now. It sounds as though she's working hard for her exams. You must be very proud of your family.'

'I am. Only — ' Margaret paused, knife held in mid-air over a waiting roll.

'Only what?'

'I wish Adam were here.' There, she'd said the words she'd been bottling up.

'You must be worried about him,' Eleanor said quietly, placing the sliced cucumber in a glass bowl with some lettuce leaves Arthur had grown in their vegetable plot at the bottom end of the garden, and tomatoes that still smelled of the greenhouse.

As if Eleanor's words had turned a key, Margaret found herself pouring out her fears.

'I feel helpless. It seems to be going badly down there. Those ships that have been sunk . . . I've stopped buying the evening paper, but when I come home on the bus the headlines are screaming at me from other passengers' copies.

'I had the afternoon off yesterday,' she went on, 'and one of the best things about it was getting home before the paper came out.

'We deliberately didn't have the television on last night, either. It's never far from my thoughts.'

She was aware of the fridge opening and closing, followed by the sound of a cork being pulled, before her boss's wife was back with two glasses of white wine, condensation already forming on the outside.

'Yet here you are, keeping everything

going, and giving your daughter a wonderful party. That takes courage. If Adam has half as much courage as you, he must be a remarkable young man.'

She raised her glass.

'Here's to Alison on her birthday. To you, for all your hard work. And to Adam, for his safe return.'

'We're planning another party when he gets back,' Margaret said, feeling more composed after they'd clinked their glasses together and she'd taken a sip of the crisp, cool wine.

'That's an excellent idea. I hope we'll be invited, if it's not too rude of me to ask. With the firm's barbecue in August, it looks as though we'll all have a lively social calendar.

'To Adam's party,' Eleanor said as they clinked glasses again. 'I'd better take this salad outside while it's nice and fresh.

'Was that a trifle I spotted in the fridge? Don't tell Clarence, or it'll disappear before anyone else gets a taste!'

Finally Arthur mastered the barbecue,

while old and young, family and friends, as well as work colleagues, mixed happily.

Margaret was pleased to see Helen looking relaxed and chatting with Eleanor. Karen was with her young man, though Margaret got the impression they weren't at ease with each other.

Paul, another solicitor at the firm, was chatting and joking and predicting that all offices would be paperless before long, thanks to technology.

'I don't like the sound of that,' she couldn't help saying as she passed by.

'Don't worry, Margaret,' Clarence reassured her. 'You'll be trained up on any new equipment and sail through, as always.'

Maybe it was tiredness as the evening went on, but occasionally she thought she glimpsed Adam among the guests out of the corner of her eye.

Once everyone was gone, Margaret was more than ready for a sit-down. Out of habit as much as anything else, she switched on the late evening news.

Any satisfaction with the day vanished. The Falklands dominated again.

Events seemed to have taken an even darker turn, with reports of a major battle raging at a place called Goose Green.

All the time they had been enjoying themselves, their son might have been in the thick of the action.

Margaret went to bed that night with a feeling of dread.

'Do you believe in premonitions?' she whispered to Arthur, after they'd switched off their bedside lights.

'No, I don't,' he replied. 'I believe in being worried and having an overactive imagination, which isn't good for anybody.'

Margaret wasn't so sure. Even with Arthur's arms around her, the sense of foreboding continued to grow and torment her in the darkness.

4

'I never realised there was all this country-side so near to the town,' Helen observed as Peter drove them past one of several local reservoirs. 'It's so peaceful, too. There's hardly any traffic.'

'That's why I brought you here,' Peter told her. 'I thought I could build up your confidence on quiet roads, as well as showing what this area has to offer.

'The moors can be a bit stark for some tastes, but they have their own beauty that gets under your skin.'

'Thank you for all the trouble you're taking to help me,' she replied. 'I wish I could return the favour.

'I've been thinking of ways to help you get back in touch with your family that wouldn't end up with you and your father arguing again. Perhaps you could go about it in the same way as you're doing this, with gradual steps.'

By now they'd come back to the out-skirts of the town. Peter indicated before pulling into the car park of a stone-built pub, cheerfully adorned with window-boxes of scarlet geraniums blazing in the Saturday sunshine.

'Why don't we talk about it over some lunch?'

Soon they were tucking into beef sand-wiches the size of doorsteps at a corner table by a window overlooking the hills.

'Your mum's the best person to ap-proach, so that she can take the matter up with your father when he's in a good mood,' Helen suggested. 'Maybe your dad regrets his actions but needs a way he can step down without wounding his pride.'

'There's my pride, too, you know,' Peter protested.

Helen sighed.

'Men! That's another reason to take it gradually, rather than risking confronta-tion. Can you arrange to meet your mother on neutral ground during the day, where your father's not likely to come across you?'

Peter looked thoughtful.

'There's a nice market town about twelve miles away that has several cafés. Helen, you're a genius.' He grinned as they clinked their glasses.

'You know, with the evenings getting lighter, if your confidence keeps improving, we'll be able to venture further afield. I know somewhere we can have a meal and a drink with an incredible sunset view.'

That last sentence was the worst thing he could have said. Helen stiffened.

'What's wrong?' Peter asked.

'Nothing.'

'There is. You can't pull the wool over my eyes.'

She put her glass down.

'It was over a drink, while watching a sunset, that I told Tony we didn't have a future together. We crashed on the drive back.'

Peter frowned.

'You can't keep blaming yourself for

what happened.'

'Yes, I can. I should have waited. I meant to leave it till later, but he was going on about the romantic sunset, getting carried away and making so many ambitious plans, I couldn't keep it back. He went from happy to upset and angry.

'I was going to phone for a taxi, but he insisted on driving me home. He drove too fast, wasn't paying attention because he kept asking me questions, and ran into another car when it braked suddenly in front of us.' She shook her head. 'I should have waited till he'd dropped me off at home.'

'But then he could have crashed just as easily on the way back to his place.'

'Maybe.' She picked up a beer mat and started ripping little pieces from the edges. 'I'd thought of going round to his place to tell him, but couldn't pluck up the courage.

'Instead, I dropped the bombshell on what was supposed to be a romantic evening.' Tears pricked the back of her eyes. 'Now you know the full story of what happened, I won't blame you if you want to walk away.'

She tensed, bracing herself for him to leave. Instead, Peter sat back, folded his arms and fixed her in a steady gaze that reminded her of someone, but she couldn't think who.

'If you think you're getting rid of me that easily, you can think again.'

★　★　★

Lunch hour in a staid solicitors' office would normally be regarded as an unlikely scene for the popping of champagne corks, even in the middle of June, but that was exactly what was happening in the wood-panelled library at Barnes and Son a couple of weeks later.

Margaret had certainly known nothing like it in all the years she had worked there, and could hardly believe it was happening.

Nor could she believe the words Clarence Barnes was saying even now as he proposed a toast.

'Here's to the end of the Falklands conflict, and the safe voyage home of Margaret's son Adam. I'd like to take this opportunity to express our thanks and appreciation for the part he and other members of the Armed Forces have played in bringing this conclusion.'

As everyone raised their glasses, bought specially by Clarence that morning in the town's only department store, Margaret remembered her tears of relief at first hearing the announcement of Argentina's surrender on the news.

'See?' Arthur had told her, referring to the premonitions that had haunted her over the past weeks. 'What did I tell you? You and your over-active imagination!'

Despite his scoffing, he hadn't been able to hide the tremor in his voice, betraying his real emotions.

After lunch the work day went on as normal, with Margaret fielding clients' phone calls and typing documents.

'Do you know when Adam will be back?' Mr Clarence asked when she took the day's letters to him to sign.

'Not really. I suppose everything's still at sixes and sevens down there with a lot to sort out, and then it will be a fair old voyage back.'

'Well, if he can make it back in time for the August barbecue, we'll be very pleased to see him.'

The barbecue, held every summer at Clarence Barnes's old stone farmhouse near the edge of the moors for the staff and their families, was always eagerly anticipated.

'Thank you,' Margaret replied. 'I hope you're prepared for him to eat you out of house and home.'

'If you ask me, he deserves every bite.' He paused. 'It looks as if we might be having a wanderer returning to the fold, too.

'Peter and Eleanor have been in touch with each other, building bridges, apparently. My wife and daughter can both be very persuasive, to the point that they've got me to consent to Peter coming for dinner on Sunday.

'Eleanor tells me he has a new girlfriend he seems keen on, though he's not ready to introduce us to her yet.'

'That's wonderful news,' Margaret couldn't help saying.

'I suppose so. Harsh words were said. Still, I don't want the situation to end as it did with my father and brother. If Peter is set on doing things a different way, I'll have to accept it.'

'While we're being honest, Mr Clarence, if there's one thing these last few weeks have taught me, it's that people putting their differences behind them would make the world a better place,' Margaret put in.

'They've also taught me that, however much grief and worry our families might cause us, they still provide support through hard times.'

She folded the last of the signed letters and slid it into its envelope as her boss replaced the cap on his fountain pen.

'Wise words, Margaret. I've come to the conclusion that I need to spend more time with my family and delegate more work to Paul.

'After all, he's more than capable. Helen's coming along nicely, too. It's good to have some new blood in the firm, even if my father might have disapproved.'

'I wouldn't be so sure about that,' Margaret replied. 'Old Mr Barnes would have been shrewd enough to move with the times, and probably glad that his son was able to learn from his mistakes.'

★   ★   ★

'How was the Sunday dinner?' Helen asked Peter one evening the following week as they enjoyed a walk round one of the reservoirs. 'You don't look too shell-shocked, so hopefully it wasn't a disaster.'

'I don't think I've ever been as nervous as I was when I rang that bell. It was my sister who opened the door.' Peter's eyes crinkled.

'She threw her arms round me and practically hung from my neck.' He cleared his throat. 'Mum pecked me on the cheek as if it was a normal Sunday dinner. Then I saw Dad, standing there as if biding his time.'

'And?' Helen asked as Peter stopped.

'You could almost have cut the air with a knife. Then he stepped forward, shook hands and said, 'I could do with a sherry. Anyone else fancy one?', and it was as if everything was back to normal. There were some tricky moments, but Mum smoothed them over.'

'So it went better than you expected? I'm so pleased for you.'

'I could hardly believe it. Even though there were no big apologies, I could tell Dad was quite emotional in his own buttoned-up way.

'Normally he's obsessed with his work, but he hardly talked about that at all.' He turned to Helen and took her hand. 'If I hadn't met you, this wouldn't have come about. Or at least not for a long while.'

He pulled her to him and kissed the top of her head.

As they stood in silence, a pair of swans floated by with a clutch of cygnets in tow. The setting sun cast a sheen across the surface of the water and lit up the nearby moors, making them glow.

At moments like this, Helen understood how people loved this landscape.

'Promise me you'll never change,' Peter murmured. 'My father and grandfather both ended up being so repressed.

'Sometimes I wonder whether the legal profession does that after a while. Maybe that's why Uncle James went away. Hopefully it won't have the same effect on you. I can't imagine you being like that.'

Helen stepped back as his words sank in.

'What exactly does your father do?'

'He's a solicitor. A senior partner, in fact. Hence all the pressure.'

She hardly dared ask the next question.

'What's he called?'

She thought of the two solicitors she'd noticed sneering at her in the county court in her early days and shuddered at the possibility that it might be one of them.

The answer was even worse.

'Clarence Barnes.'

Her stomach clenched.

'But when we first met you said your surname was Barker.'

'No. Barnes. You probably didn't hear me properly. The music was rather loud.'

'And I'm obviously no good at lip-reading.' Helen shook her head. 'When you mentioned a family firm, I assumed something in engineering or sales.'

'There are a lot of small businesses like that around here. I thought it might be in the next town, as that's where you're living. But you know what my job is.'

'So you've come across my father?' he asked.

'More than that. I work for him.'

It was Peter's turn to be shocked.

'Didn't you put two and two together? Or even think to ask?' Helen cried.

'There's no need to shout. First, you know I didn't particularly want to talk about my past. Second, your firm sounded larger and more modern.

'Ours is only small. I'd never have thought they'd take on someone like you.'

'It's expanded in the last few years. And what do you mean by someone like me?'

'Sorry.' Peter put his hands to his head. 'Believe me, that last remark wasn't a reflection on you.'

Helen felt the surge of anger pass, but her heart was still pounding.

'This is terrible. Your father's brilliant in many ways, but he's still very old school in others. How's he going to react to one of his employees going out with his son?' she went on. 'Suppose I have to choose between seeing you or keeping my job? Just when things seemed to be settling down — '

'I'm sure it won't come to that.' Peter

took a deep breath. 'We'll keep it quiet to be on the safe side. We won't tell my parents until we're ready to take that step and you're established with the firm.'

Still, Helen couldn't help worrying. No-one was indispensable, and secrecy might even make matters worse in the long run, especially if someone felt he'd been deceived.

She had already had one bad experience of Clarence Barnes's controlled anger after a serious error during her first week.

That had been bad enough, but something told her it might be nothing compared to this.

★   ★   ★

Matters came to a head sooner than either of them anticipated after barely a fortnight, when Peter drove Helen home after a meal in an Indian restaurant to celebrate their three-month anniversary.

They'd been travelling for a few minutes when Helen noticed he'd steered wide round a bend. That was unusual for him. He was such a careful driver.

'Are you OK?' she asked.

Peter gave a wan smile.

'I feel a bit odd. Maybe I shouldn't have chosen the prawn curry.'

'Sometimes there's a good reason for playing it safe,' Helen agreed, not mentioning the way he'd teased her for choosing a mild dish. She looked more closely at him. 'You're breaking out in a sweat. Are you sure you're well enough to drive?'

'I'll be fine.' He swallowed. 'On second thoughts, maybe I won't. We need to pull over.'

Luckily there was plenty of room at the side of the road. The car ended up at a slight angle, but it was out of the way of the traffic.

It was only when the car came to a standstill and Peter rested his forehead on the steering wheel that Helen realised how much she was shaking.

She refused to let herself think what might have happened if Peter had tried to drive further, or if he had been taken ill nearer the town centre, with lanes and traffic lights to contend with. As she knew only too well, the worst could happen within seconds.

She pushed the memory out of her mind and forced herself to concentrate on helping Peter, now grimacing with pain and holding his arms over his stomach.

'I'll call an ambulance.'

'There's no need. It's only a bug. Anyway, how could you phone anyone?'

She glanced around. There was no sign of a phone box. A few large houses, all with forbidding-looking front gardens separated from the pavement by gates and shrubs, lined the road.

'I'll knock at a door and ask to use their phone.'

'That won't go down well at this time of night.'

'It's only half past nine.'

Even as she protested, she could see his point. There were hardly any lights on, making most of the houses seem deserted.

'You can't stay here. I could drive you home. I'm out of practice, but I should be able to manage.'

'You're not insured. If the police stopped you, you could get into trouble.'

'In that case, I'd better phone from one of these houses, or walk till I find a phone box.'

'Write this number down,' Peter said as if hearing her silent question.

She wrote the number he recited to her in her diary.

'Whose is it?'

'My mum's.'

Helen froze.

'Her home number?'

Peter nodded before grimacing again.

'She's usually the one who answers, so it should be OK.' He tried to laugh. 'If my dad does answer, you could always put on a foreign accent and pretend to be somebody else.'

After running up the drive of the nearest house that had lights on and ringing the doorbell, Helen shivered on the step for a couple of minutes before there was the sound of a chain being slotted into place.

The door opened a fraction and a man's face peered out. When she explained the situation, his expression turned to one of understanding.

'If there's a phone box nearby, I'll use that if you can give me directions. I've got plenty of change,' she finished.

'No need for that,' the man assured her. 'The nearest one is a good walk away, and we don't want a lass like you wandering round on her own in the dark. Come on in. Our phone's just in the hall.'

Barely aware of her surroundings, Helen checked the number she'd written down. Would an ambulance be better, despite Peter's insistence to the contrary? It would help to avoid a confrontation with his parents.

Fingers trembling, she started dialling, hoping she was making the right decision.

★   ★   ★

Clarence was in his study when he heard the phone. He frowned. He'd always made sure their home number was ex-directory.

Most people who did have it would hardly be calling at — he glanced at the clock on the mantelpiece — quarter to ten, which made it somewhat concerning that they should be ringing now.

Pushing the papers he'd been working on to one side, he'd just stood up when it stopped and he heard Eleanor's voice.

'Oh, no,' she said after a gap. 'Where are you?'

Clarence got to the hall as his wife jotted something down on a notepad.

'Don't worry,' she said, widening her eyes at him. 'We'll be with you in a few minutes.'

His chest tightened.

'What's happened?'

'It's Peter. He's come down with some sort of illness while driving a friend home and isn't well enough to continue. He wouldn't hear of an ambulance, so she's called us.'

'She?'

He didn't get an answer as his wife concentrated more than seemed necessary on tearing the page off the pad.

The grandfather clock ticked loudly in the brief silence as her eyes flickered towards the stairs where Samantha was sitting.

'Is Peter all right?'

'Your brother's poorly and needs us to collect him. Honestly, it's just like when he was a boy and the school used to phone me to fetch him home.' Eleanor laughed unconvincingly. 'Will you be all right on your own for an hour?'

'I should be. Longer, if he needs to go to hospital.'

Even in the tension of the moment, Clarence was impressed by how sensible Sam was being. His daughter was growing up fast.

'In that event, one of us will take him and the other come back here,' he replied, already lifting the keys to the BMW off the hook. 'It's all in hand.'

As they sped to the address Eleanor had written down, Clarence had to make a conscious effort not to grip the steering wheel too tightly. Eleanor, in the passenger seat, had a folded blanket on her lap.

'It sounds like it's maybe something he ate, as they'd just been for a meal.' She hesitated. 'Clarence, about the girl who phoned. Promise me you'll keep your cool.'

'What do you mean?'

'I think you know. Oh, there's Peter's car. Just remember what I've said.'

As they drew up, it was probably as well that Clarence had already come to a stop before he saw the pale face of the woman standing next to it. A steely coldness stole through him as realisation dawned.

'Why are you here?'

Despite his anger, he felt uncomfortable as Helen flinched at his tone.

'I thought I should watch for you arriving. Peter's inside the house. The couple who kindly let me use their phone reckoned he'd be better off there.'

Eleanor was already halfway up the

112

path. Clarence followed her, with Helen bringing up the rear.

⋆　⋆　⋆

'He should recover here,' Dr Beresford, the family's general practitioner, reassured them an hour later at home. An old family friend, he had come round even though he wasn't on call.

'He'll need a couple of days' rest. Give him fluids for the next twenty-four hours, and a light diet after that.'

When they had collected Peter, Clarence's practical side had taken over, and he'd driven Peter's car, with Helen in the back with the patient, while Eleanor drove the BMW.

After that, Helen had stayed mostly in the background, turning down Eleanor's offer of a lift and leaving in a taxi once she knew Peter would recover.

Now, with their son asleep and Sam also having settled down, Clarence's anger, which had faded while other matters took priority, boiled over.

'No wonder he was coy about the identity of this girlfriend he mentioned. She's just as bad, seeing him all this time and deceiving me every day in the process.'

'Oh, for goodness' sake, Clarence,' Eleanor snapped. 'They're both adults and entitled to see whomever they like.

'In fact, from what Peter's just been able to tell me, neither of them realised the connection until recently. Apparently Helen was aghast when she found out, worried about her job.'

'So she should be. The match is entirely unsuitable. How can an employee of a firm go out with the owner's son?'

'Perfectly easily, I should think,' his wife retorted. 'Bear in mind that Helen started off with fewer advantages than Peter but finished her degree and went on to qualify.' She sighed.

'You might not have been aware of the full extent of your father's hostility towards me the first few times you brought me here, but I certainly was.

'He described me as only a nurse and

made it clear that he expected you to marry someone more suitable.'

'This is different,' Clarence argued, knowing deep down that she was right but unable to back down. 'My father didn't see you around the office every day. He wasn't your boss. How am I supposed to react to her when I see her at work?'

'As you would to anyone else.' They looked round to see Peter, pale and shaking, leaning against the door frame. 'You'd better get used to it, Dad, because I love Helen and I'm not going to give her up.'

*　*　*

'How quickly the nights are drawing in.' Helen sighed. 'Sometimes it seems we've hardly got used to the lighter evenings before they start fading away again.

'Which is all the more reason for us to make the most of them,' she added.

August had come round and, with it, the night of the firm's summer party.

Apart from the progress of Margaret's son's voyage home from the Falklands, everyone at work seemed to have talked about nothing else over the past weeks.

'There's always been a summer party, even when I started, back in old Mr Barnes's day. It's a wonderful occasion, definitely not to be missed,' Margaret had told Helen.

'Much bigger than the one I had at my house in May. Mr Clarence's house and garden are huge, so there's plenty of room. He even dons an apron and mans the barbecue.'

That was where Helen and Peter were heading now, stopping off on the way to give a lift to Karen, the firm's junior secretary, nervous of turning up by herself after splitting up with her boyfriend when they'd been on the point of getting engaged.

'I remembered what you said to me about being sure what I wanted before getting in too deep,' she'd confided in Helen. 'When I said that I didn't want to get engaged, he seemed relieved.

Anyway, we had a proper talk and agreed to call it a day.'

Karen was waiting for them on the pavement, wearing a pretty, dark red dress.

'What if no-one talks to me?' she fretted as she got in. 'I bet I'm the only one there on their own.'

'We'll talk to you, and so will a lot of other people,' Helen told her. 'It isn't as though you don't know anybody.'

When they arrived, Helen suddenly realised she hadn't had even a moment's anxiety on the journey.

'The next time we visit, I might be driving,' she said to Peter. 'I'll have my own car by then.'

The old house stood, solid and reassuring, against the backdrop of the moors. Fairy lights hung from the trees in the small orchard, while roses and honeysuckle scented the air.

Helen gasped at the sight of trestle tables covered with white linen cloths and laden with sumptuous-looking dishes.

'We'll never get through all that.'

'Oh, you'd be surprised,' Eleanor replied, embracing all three of them in turn when they reached the house. 'The fresh air up here engenders a healthy appetite.

'Now, if you want anything from the barbecue, I suggest you go over and get your order in. Clarence has got it all in hand, but some of these things take time to cook and he's already inundated.'

'Who's that with Margaret?' Karen asked as they made their way past the conservatory, greeting other guests as they went.

Helen looked in the direction she was nodding and recognised Margaret's husband and daughter, who was wearing the puffball dress she'd worn at her birthday party and which Margaret had joked she would sleep in, given half a chance. A well-built young man stood with them.

'That must be Adam.'

Margaret had travelled down to Portsmouth the previous week for the homecoming of her son's ship. Back at work, she'd described some of the many emotional scenes that had taken place.

'I'm glad I went,' she'd said. 'It just felt so right to be there. I'll never forget it as long as I live.'

Now, catching sight of their little group, she waved them over.

'Come and meet my son,' she told them, beaming with pride and relief.

Adam was polite yet quiet, as if not quite comfortable in these circles.

His eyes lit up, though, when he met Karen, while something about the way she drew herself up just that little bit taller hinted at a spark between them.

From the knowing way that she smiled, Margaret had clearly noticed it, too.

Clarence Barnes, skilfully flipping burgers and sausages on a large barbecue, looked up as Helen and Peter approached.

'Ah, here you are. What would you like? I recommend the lamb burgers, supplied by one of the local farmers. If you want to sit down, my able assistant Samantha will bring them over when they're ready.'

Sam waved from where she was standing with her mum a few yards away.

Helen still felt nervous in his presence. After the incident with Peter's sudden illness, she had been almost too scared to go to work the next day, still shaking when she arrived and was told that Mr Clarence wanted to see her in his office.

'I can't pretend this is easy for either of us,' he had said, sitting behind his huge mahogany desk, fingers steepled.

'However, Peter has convinced me both of his course of action and of your sincerity. Mistakes have been made in the past, but rest assured that your job here is secure.'

He had added that Helen had his blessing to keep seeing Peter, but that private and professional life should be kept separate — something with which she heartily agreed.

A nudge from Peter brought her back to the present.

'See the sawn-off branch on that beech tree? That broke when I was trying to build a treehouse for Sam. I ended up with my arm in plaster. The treehouse never got built.

'Rather than risk the same thing happening again, Mum and Dad had the summerhouse at the end of the garden renovated. It was practically falling down before then,' he added, leading her to a hexagonal dark wooden building with green and white window frames.

When they stepped in and shut the door, the noise of the party faded as they became enclosed in their own little world.

Out of the windows to one side, the last of the sun peered over the moors. The other side looked over the garden that held the memories of generations.

'Dad told me recently that he and Uncle James used to love dreaming in here, too. It was their den. That's why he made sure to keep its old character. Now it's better than ever. Just like my life at this moment.'

'And mine,' Helen agreed.

Even as they kissed and she sensed

the past and its problems fading behind them, she knew that coming to the area and making a fresh start had turned out to be the best thing she had ever done.

More than that, she looked forward to following the path that lay before them and seeing what the future held, for her, Peter, and everyone else who was here.